A Frog in the Bog

To my wonderful agent, Steve, who helped me make it in the frog-eat-bug world of writing
—K. W.

For Lana and Chris. In memory of your childhood
—J. R.

ALADDIN PAPERBACKS

An imprint of Simon & Schuster Children's Publishing Division

1230 Avenue of the Americas, New York, NY 10020

Text copyright © 2003 by Karma Wilson

Illustrations copyright © 2003 by Joan Rankin

ALADDIN PAPERBACKS and colophon are trademarks of Simon & Schuster, Inc.

Also available in a Margaret K. McElderry Books hardcover edition.

Designed by Kristin Smith

The text of this book was set in Gorilla.

The illustrations for this book were rendered in watercolor.

Manufactured in China

First Aladdin Paperbacks edition February 2007

16 18 20 19 17 15

The Library of Congress has cataloged the hardcover edition as follows:

Wilson, Karma.

A Frog in the Bog / Karma Wilson ; illustrated by Joan Rankin.

p. cm.

Summary: A frog in the bog grows larger and larger as he eats more and more bugs,
until he attracts the attention of an alligator who puts an end to his eating.

ISBN-13: 978-0-689-84081-4 (hc)

ISBN-10: 0-689-84081-0 (hc)

[1. Frogs—Fiction. 2. Insects—Fiction. 3. Alligators—Fiction. 4. Stories in rhyme.]

I. Rankin, Joan, ill. II. Title.

PZ8.3.W6976 On 2003

[E]—dc21

2002005903

ISBN-13: 978-1-4169-2727-3 (pbk)

ISBN-10: 1-4169-2727-1 (pbk)

0219 SCP

karma wilson

joan rankin

A Frog
in the Bog

Aladdin Paperbacks · NEW YORK LONDON TORONTO SYDNEY

There's a frog on the log in the middle of the bog.

A small, green frog
on a half-sunk log
in the middle of the bog.

He flicks ONE tick
as it creeps up a stick.

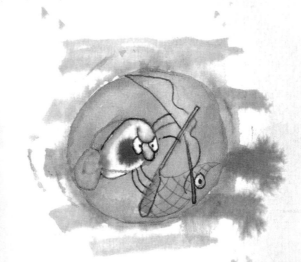

ONE tick in the belly of a small, green frog

on a half-sunk log

in the middle of the bog.

And the frog grows
a little bit
bigger. . . .

He sees TWO fleas
as they leap through the reeds.

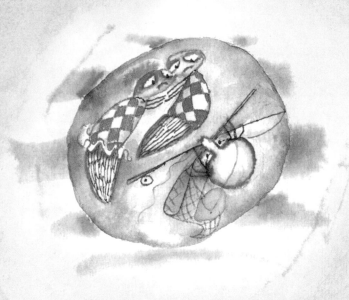

ONE tick, **TWO** fleas
in the belly of the frog
on a half-sunk log
in the middle of the bog.

And the frog grows
a little bit
bigger. . . .

flyrodrome

He spies THREE flies
as they buzz through the skies.

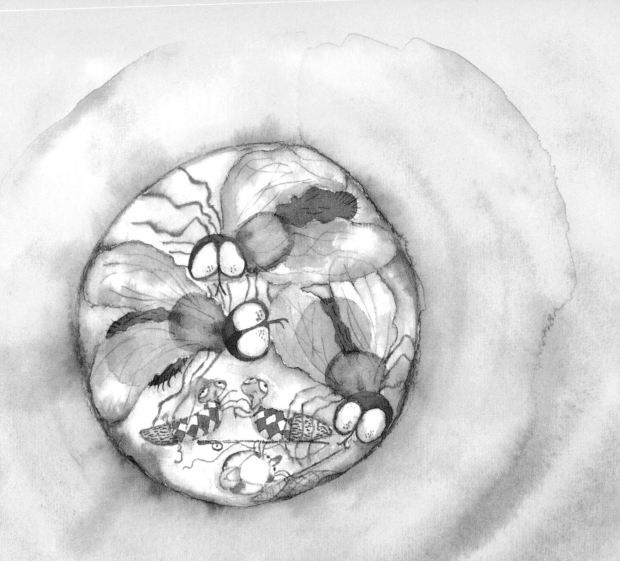

ONE tick, **TWO** fleas, **THREE** flies (Oh, my!)
in the belly of the frog
on a half-sunk log
in the middle of the bog.

And the frog grows
a little bit
bigger. . . .

He glugs FOUR slugs
as they slink through the sludge.

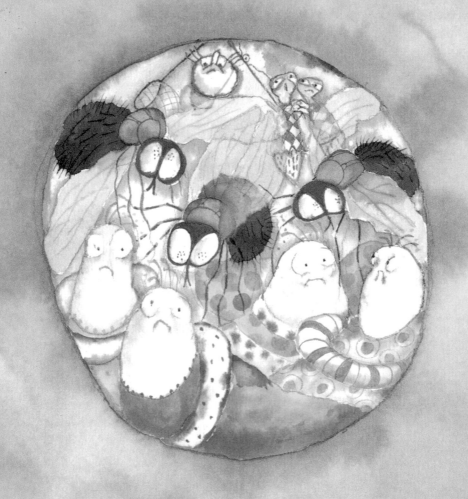

ONE tick, **TWO** fleas, **THREE** flies (Oh, my!),

FOUR slugs (Ew, ugh!) in the belly of the frog

on a half-sunk log

in the middle of the bog.

And the frog grows
a little bit
bigger. . . .

He inhales FIVE snails
from their heads to their tails!

ONE tick, TWO fleas, THREE flies (Oh, my!),
FOUR slugs (Ew, ugh!), and FIVE slimy snails
in the belly of the frog
on a half-sunk log
in the middle of the bog.

What a hog, that frog!

that log with the frog
in the middle of the bog
starts to rise . . .

and the frog sees eyes!

And the frog sees claws
and a big set of jaws,
and a mouth like a crater!
And the frog screams,

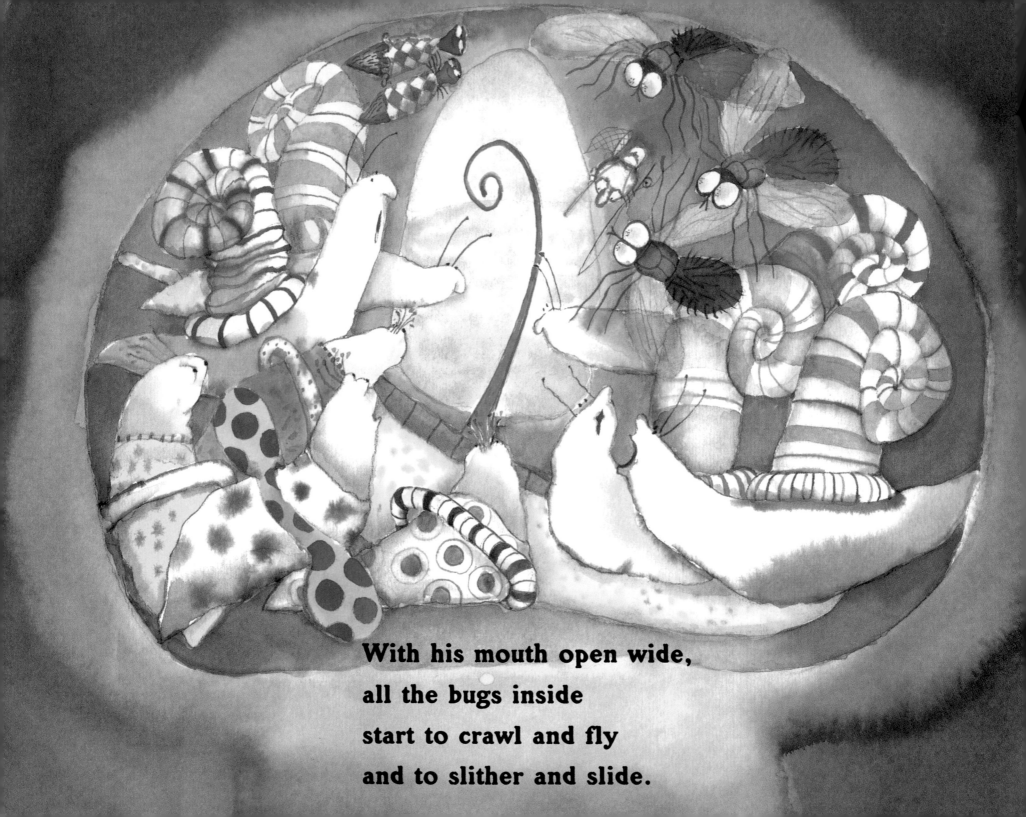

With his mouth open wide,
all the bugs inside
start to crawl and fly
and to slither and slide.

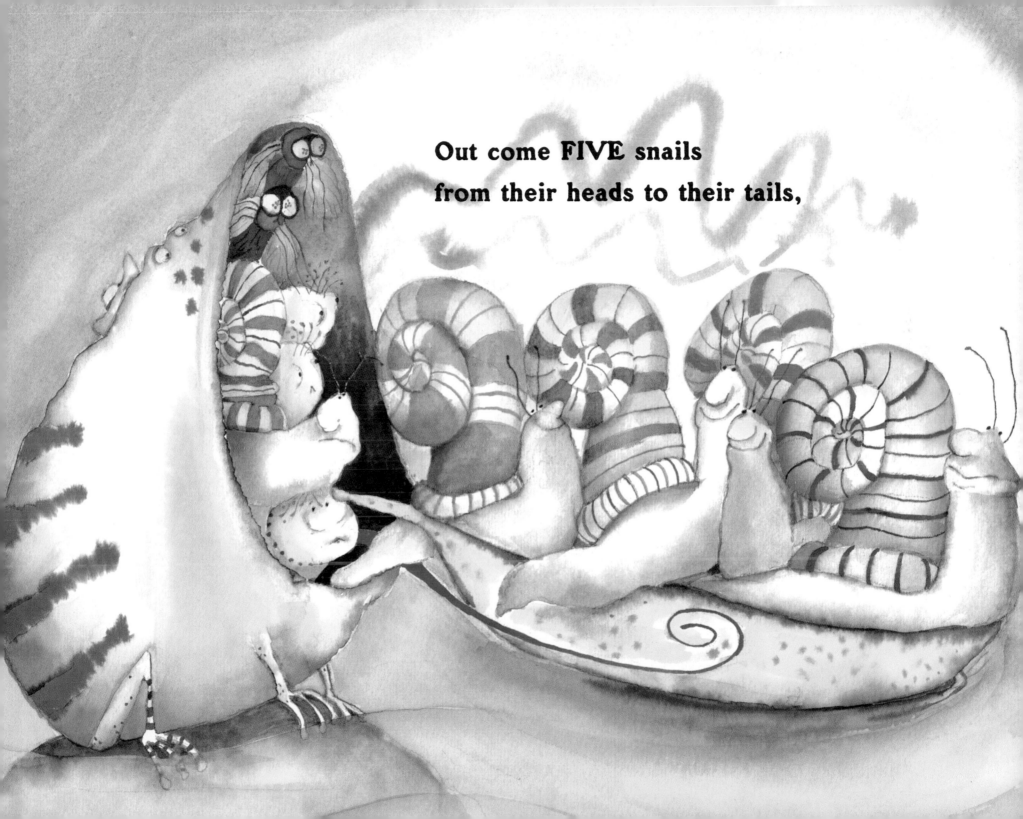

Out come **FIVE** snails
from their heads to their tails,

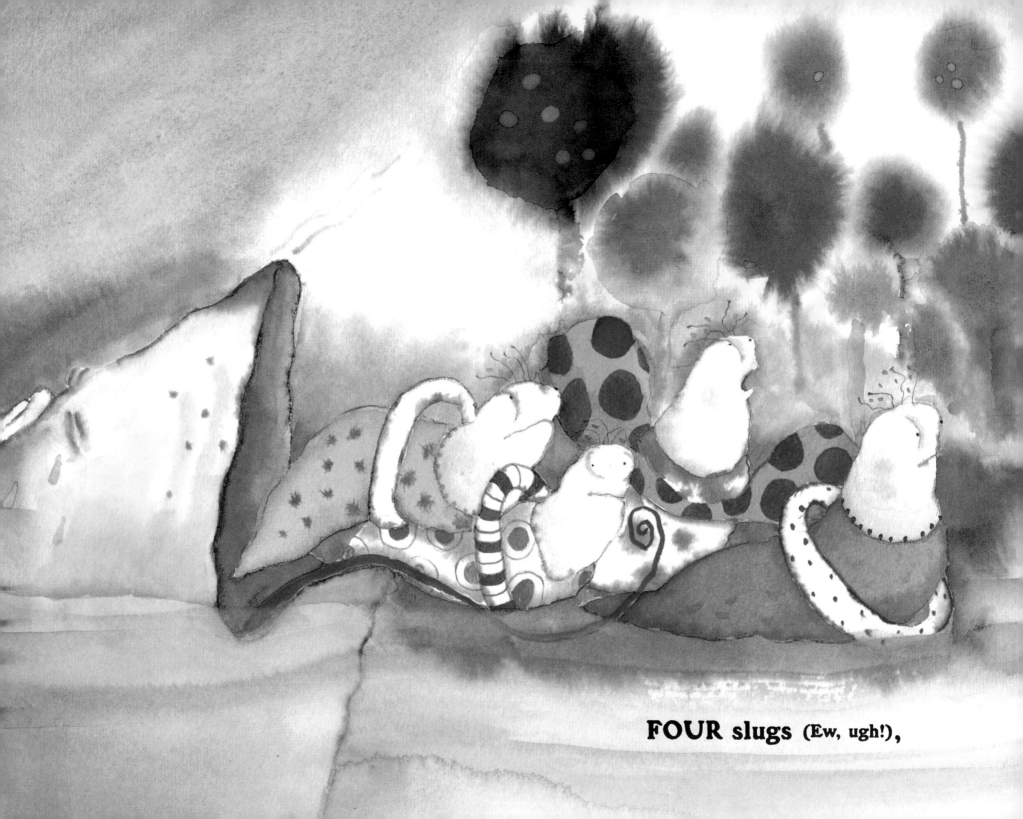

FOUR slugs (Ew, ugh!),

TWO fleas (Dear me!),

and ONE tiny tick.

ICK!

And right in the middle of his holler,

that frog grows
a whole lot
smaller. . . .

"See ya later," says the gator
as he romps through the swamp,
cuz the itty-bitty frog
isn't big enough to chomp.

Now . . .

the bugs in the bog
keep away from the frog,

and the frog NEVER sits on a half-sunk log!